Merry Christmas
To
`Robert
from
Grandma & Grandpa
12/25/75

When the Wild Ducks Come

A FOLLETT BEGINNING-TO-READ BOOK

When the Wild Ducks Come

Margaret Chittenden

Illustrated by Beatrice Darwin

FOLLETT PUBLISHING COMPANY
Chicago

Library of Congress Catalog Card Number: 74-187122

ISBN 695-80348-4   trade binding
ISBN 695-40348-0   titan binding

First Printing

I know when spring is here.

Bright green leaf buds come out on the branches of the oak trees.

Under the boughs, white daisies spread across the new grass like stars.

Squirrels run up and down the trunks of the oak trees. They chatter and scold one another and me.

Then the wild ducks come. Two of them.
I see them high in the sky coming closer and
closer. They land on the daisy-scattered grass
beneath the oak trees.

The male duck is gray with a white tail. His green-black head shines in the sun as he watches over the female duck.

8

Her feathers are brown and black with touches of white.

The male duck stands guard while the female eats pieces of bread I have scattered under the trees.

He watches while she rests. He does not eat or rest.

My cat creeps across the soft grass.

The male duck cries a warning and both ducks fly away.

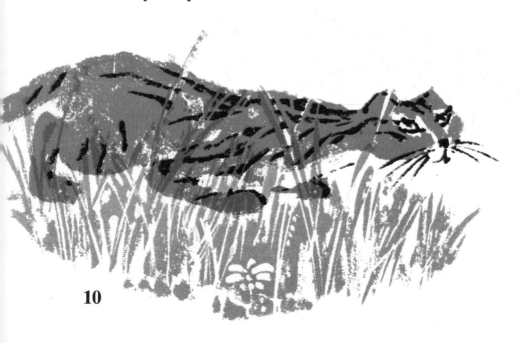

For several weeks the ducks come to
breakfast on the grass under the oak trees.

I know when summer comes.

Rose petals drift across the grass under the
oak trees.

12

After a summer rain, the pine trees are clean
and fluffy, as though each needle had been
combed into place.

Woolly bear caterpillars hump their backs
when I find them under leaves.

The wild ducks build their home by the pond nearby.

The nest is lined with down from the female.

There are eight pale green eggs in the nest.
After a few weeks, eight downy brown and
yellow bodies wriggle and squirm in the nest.

Eight little mouths chirp and peep. Eight yellow bills open wide for tender worms. Every day the mother duck finds food for her babies.

I know when fall is here.

The maple trees paint the grass with red,
yellow, and orange leaves.

18

The fallen leaves crunch and crackle when I walk on the grass under the trees.

Spiky cones grow on the pine trees and the squirrels run faster, gathering nuts for winter food.

Down at the pond, the baby ducks grow
bigger. Every day their wings grow stronger.

They flap their wings and follow their mother and father. They soar a little further each day into the endless blue of the fall sky.

I know when winter comes.

The pine cones fall from the trees, and green-brown needles carpet the grass under the pines.

We bring logs and build a fire in the fireplace.

We stare into the orange-red flames,
wondering when the snow will come.

One day the sky is filled with long lines of
flying ducks.

26

They beat their wings up and down, up and down. They follow their leader, heading south before the snow comes.

There are no ducks now at the pond. I am sad that they have gone.

Then I remember that spring will come again
and the wild ducks will return.

Next year and every year, the wild ducks
will come again.

When the Wild Ducks Come

Reading Level: Level Two. *When the Wild Ducks Come* has a total vocabulary of 202 words. It has been tested in second-grade classes, where it was read with ease.

Uses of the Book: Reading for fun. This word picture of the coming and going of the seasons and a family of ducks incites the rich imaginations of children.

Word List

All of the 202 words used in *When the Wild Ducks Come* are listed. Regular verb forms and plurals of words already on the list are not listed separately, but the endings are given in parentheses after the word.

5	I		daisy (ies)		high
	know		spread		in
	when		across		sky
	spring		new		close (r)
	is		grass		land
	here		like		scatter (ed)
	bright		star (s)	8	male
	green	6	squirrel (s)		gray
	leaf		run		with
	bud (s)		up		tail
	come (ing)		and		his
	out		down		black
	on		trunk (s)		head (ing)
	the		they		shine (s)
	branch (es)		chatter		sun
	of		scold		as
	oak		one		he
	tree (s)		another		watch (es)
	under		me		over
	bough (s)	7	then		female
	white		wild		her
			duck (s)		feather (s)
			two		are
			see		brown
			them		touch (es)

30

9 stand (s)	caterpillar (s)	cone (s)
guard	hump	grow
while	their	fast (er)
eat (s)	back (s)	gather (ing)
piece (s)	find	nut (s)
bread	15 build	winter
have	home	21 big (ger)
she	by	wing (s)
rest (s)	pond	strong (er)
does	nearby	22 flap
not	nest	follow
10 my	line (d, s)	father
cat	from	soar
creep (s)	16 there	further
soft	eight	endless
cry (ies)	pale	blue
warn (ing)	egg (s)	23 carpet
both	few	24 we
fly (ing)	yellow	bring
away	body (ies)	log (s)
11 for	wriggle	fire (place)
several	squirm	25 stare
week (s)	17 little	wonder (ing)
to	mouth (s)	snow
breakfast	chirp	26 fill (ed)
12 summer	peep	long
rose	bill (s)	27 beat
petal (s)	open	lead (er)
drift	wide	head (ing)
13 after	tender	south
rain	worm (s)	before
pine	every	28 no
clean	day	now
fluffy	mother	am
though	food	sad
each	18 fall (en)	that
needle (s)	maple	gone
had	paint	29 remember
been	red	will
comb (ed)	orange	again
into	19 crunch	return
place	crackle	next
14 woolly	walk	year
bear	20 spiky	